The King

by Bobby Lynn Maslen
pictures by John R. Maslen

Scholastic Inc.
New York • Toronto • London • Auckland • Sydney • Mexico City • New Delhi • Hong Kong • Buenos Aires

Available Bob Books®:

Set 1: Beginning Readers
Set 2: Advancing Beginners
Set 3: Word Families
Set 4: Complex Words
Set 5: Long Vowels

Ask for Bob Books at your local bookstore, or visit www.bobbooks.com.

ISBN 0-439-17591-7

20 19 18   17 18 19 20/0

Printed in China
This edition first printing, May 2006

In the spring, the king sang
a ringing song.

"Bang the gong, clang the clong, sing the song," sang the king.

So the bell did ring and the gong did clang, and the king, with his song, was happy in the spring.

In the happy kingdom there was a sad, mad girl.
When the king passed, she frowned and stamped her foot.

She did not smile. She did
not like his song. She did
not say, "Long live the King!"

The king was sad.
The king went to bed.

The king did not feel happy.
He did not feel proud.

On the hilltop the king sang
a sad song.

"Ding-dong, bing-bong, wrong-wrong," he sang. The notes were bad. The music was sad.

The little girl was mad. She said with glee, "The king does not sing all because of ME!"

The king was wise and seldom wrong. "Find the girl and bring her along", he told his best man in a tone quite strong.

His man went to the girl. He said
in a tone very strong, "The king
wants you to come along!"

So the little girl went to see the king.

Her lips were down in a frown. Her cheeks were red. She felt a little silly, but still she was mad.

"What is wrong?" said the king.
"Why are you sad?"

The little girl answered when she
saw that the king was kind,
"A friend is what I want to find."

The king was happy to hear what was wrong. "Ho-ho, Ha-ha, Ha-hee", sang the king. "That you can have, as you will see."

The king and the girl had a long
talk. They went for a walk. They
swam in the sea. They looked at
books. They looked at TV.

"Now at last we are friends," said the king with a grin. The little girl was happy to have found a friend.

So again that spring the king sang a ringing song. The girl banged the gong. She clanged the clong. She sang the song. She had a friend. It was a happy time to be at THE END.

The End

Book 8 adds:

Blends:
ing
ang
ong